Two and
Too Much

by Mildred Pitts Walter
illustrated by Pat Cummings

Bradbury Press   New York

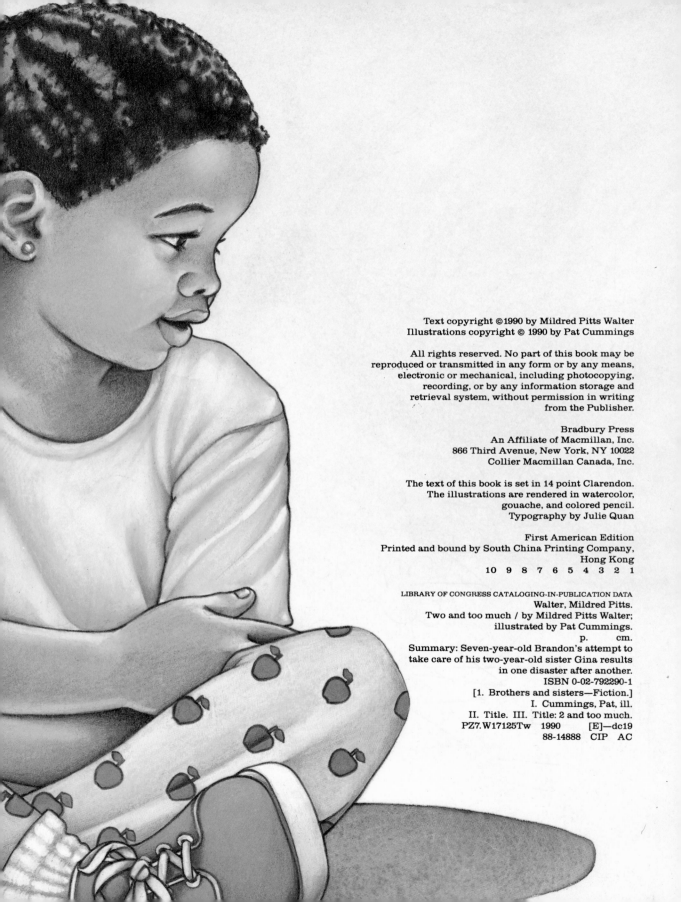

Bradbury Press
An Affiliate of Macmillan, Inc.
866 Third Avenue, New York, NY 10022
Collier Macmillan Canada, Inc.

The text of this book is set in 14 point Clarendon.
The illustrations are rendered in watercolor,
gouache, and colored pencil.
Typography by Julie Quan

First American Edition
Printed and bound by South China Printing Company,
Hong Kong
10 9 8 7 6 5 4 3 2 1

LIBRARY OF CONGRESS CATALOGING-IN-PUBLICATION DATA
Walter, Mildred Pitts.
Two and too much / by Mildred Pitts Walter;
illustrated by Pat Cummings.
p.   cm.
Summary: Seven-year-old Brandon's attempt to
take care of his two-year-old sister Gina results
in one disaster after another.
ISBN 0-02-792290-1
[1. Brothers and sisters—Fiction.]
I. Cummings, Pat, ill.
II. Title. III. Title: 2 and too much.
PZ7.W17125Tw 1990   [E]—dc19
88-14888 CIP AC

To Hadiya
—*M.P.W.*

To my dear Auntie Lea
—*P.C.*

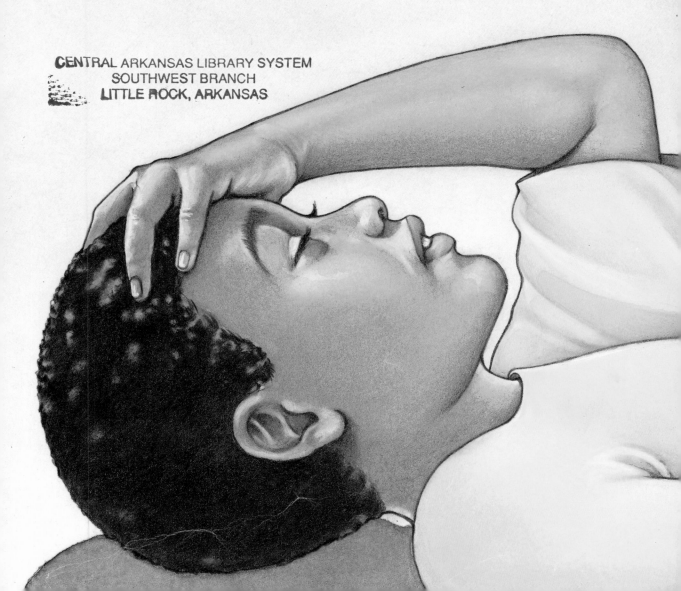

The delicious aroma of apple pie baking in the oven filled the kitchen. Brandon watched as his mama sprinkled chopped nuts on a round yellow mound of soft cheese. Gina, his baby sister, picked bits of nuts off with her little fingers and ate them.

Company was coming. Ladies only. Mama's friends. Daddy called this get-together *ladies' swap meet*. All the mamas swapped stories about their two- and three-year-olds. Brandon was glad the swap meet was at their house. Besides all the good things to eat, their neighbor Mrs. Little was coming to help clean. He could be off to play with friends today without Gina. Just as he was about to say good-bye, the phone rang.

"I get it," Gina cried.

Brandon got there first.

"No, no," Gina screamed. "I get it!"

Brandon hurriedly answered the phone. It was Mrs. Little. She asked Brandon to tell his mama that an emergency had come up. She would not be able to come.

Gina still pulled at Brandon, screaming, "I get it. I get it." When Brandon hung up the phone, she plopped to the floor, crying.

"What is it?" Mama asked, rushing into the room with the vacuum cleaner. "Why is Gina crying?"

"She wants the phone."

"Oh, Brandon, she's only two. Why couldn't she say hello?"

"It's an emergency, Mama. Mrs. Little can't come."

"Can't come! Oh, no. I'd better call her. But how will I ever get ready for company?"

Just then Brandon let out a yell: "Gina!"

Gina had unzipped the back of the bag on the vacuum cleaner. She was busy pulling fuzzy dirt onto the floor.

"No, no, Gina!" Mama shouted.

Brandon had an urge to laugh, but he said, "She needs a spanking, Mama."

"She's only two." Mama sighed.

Brandon thought his mama was about to cry. Concerned, he said, "I'll help you."

"What can you do?" Mama asked, still alarmed.

What can I do? I'm seven years old, Brandon thought. His feelings were hurt. "I can vacuum and dust," he said.

Mama looked at Gina and the mess. "Tell you what, Brandon. You take care of her, and I'll do the cleaning. Okay?"

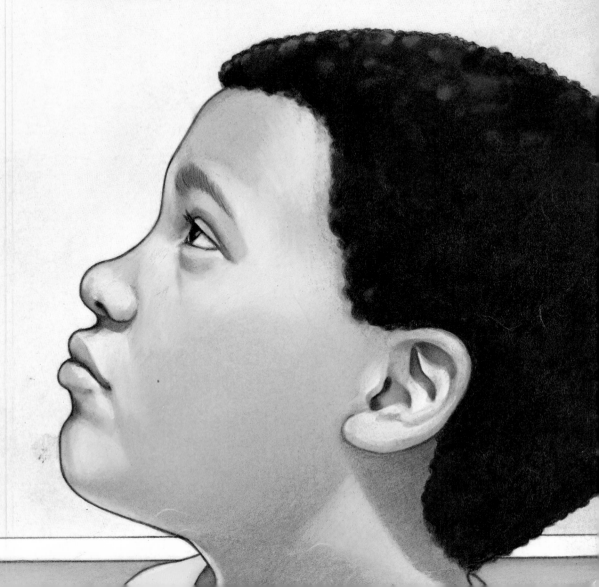

What can I do with that little girl?
Brandon wondered. Then he thought, She's
always in my room. She likes it there. He
took Gina's hand. "Want to come to my room?"

"No!" Gina said.

"Mama, she doesn't want me to take care
of her."

"Don't ask Gina what she wants to do. You
know she says *no* to everything. Just take
her and do something fun with her."

In his room Brandon let Gina make a picture. Gina worked hard and broke one of his new crayons. Brandon decided to give her the small basket of broken ones.

When Gina was finished, he knew that her picture wasn't that good, but he wanted to put it on his bulletin board. That should make her happy.

"Good girl, Gina. I'm going to hang your picture," he said.

Gina clapped her hands and laughed.

Brandon tacked the picture on the board. "You like that?" he asked. "That's pretty, huh, Gina?" He looked around, but Gina was not there. Where is she? he wondered.

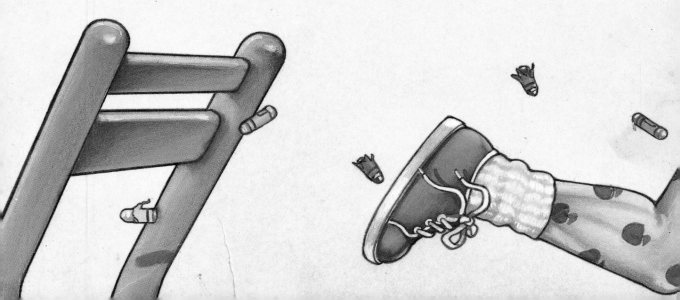

He found her sitting at their mama's dressing table with lipstick on her face. Dusting powder covered the table, and she was just about to spray herself with Mama's best perfume.

"I pretty?" Gina asked, grinning at Brandon.

"No, you're not pretty," he muttered. He didn't want their mama to hear. Mama might think he couldn't handle a two-year-old.

He looked at Gina and laughed. "You're a clown," he said, as he cleaned her face. He wiped up the powder, hoping his mother wouldn't notice. If only Gina would go to sleep. But it wasn't even lunchtime yet. Maybe she would listen to a story.

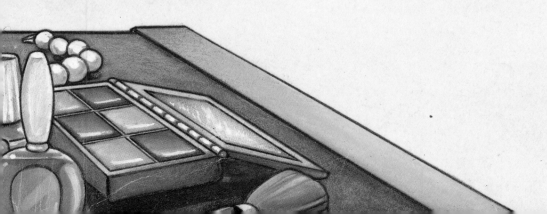

"Come choose a book, Gina," he said, leading her into his room. He was glad that his favorite book was on top of his bookshelf. She chose it.

With Gina near, Brandon stretched out to read. The story became so interesting that he forgot his little sister. Suddenly there was a loud crash. He jumped up just in time to see his cars racing all over the place. Gina had knocked over his perfect three-story garage. Oh, no, not that! Brandon thought. Why had he promised to stay home and help?

"Gina," he said angrily, "you're a bad, bad girl."

Gina screwed up her face to cry. "I not bad," she said.

"No, you're stupid." Brandon fumed, picking up the cars.

Tears rolled down Gina's face. Brandon felt sorry, but he didn't say so. Gina started to leave the room.

"Oh, no, you don't," Brandon said, closing the door. "I'm going to keep an eye on you." He got busy rebuilding his garage.

Gina stood by looking sad.

"Want to help?"

"No." Gina smiled. *No* seemed to be the only word she knew.

Just then Mama peeped into the room. "My, what a team," she said, pleased that Brandon was keeping Gina busy. "How about some lunch?"

They found milk and peanut butter and jelly sandwiches on the kitchen table. Brandon quickly ate his lunch.

Still hungry, he decided to have another sandwich and more milk. Just then he heard a sloshing sound. Milk overflowed the jelly jar onto the floor, and Gina, looking very surprised, still poured more.

"Mama!" Brandon shrieked.

"Oh, Brandon! Why did you leave the milk so close to Gina? She doesn't know any better."

I know. She's only two! he wanted to shout, but he didn't say it. He wished he had gone to play with his friends. Never again will I offer to help, he thought.

Mama washed Gina's face and hands.
"Please take her and change her clothes.
Good thing the kitchen floor has not been
cleaned."

In Gina's room he changed her clothes.
She was quiet and helpful. He left her to put
the dirty clothes away. What could he do
now to keep Gina happy?

He was in the laundry room when he had
an idea. He would play his records for her.

"Gina," he called when he reached her door. He looked in. She was nowhere in sight. Oh, no, he thought. What now? He ran from room to room.

"Gina," he called. "Where are you?" Where could she be? Brandon became frightened.

"Mama, Mama," he called. "Gina's gone."

"What do you mean, gone?" Mama asked, alarmed.

Brandon's heart beat wildly. He thought he would burst into tears. "She's not in the house," he cried.

"Oh, she has to be. Calm down, now," Mama said soothingly.

Brandon thought, Where was she last? In her room. Maybe she's hiding. He ran to Gina's room with his mama right behind him. They looked all around the room. In the closet. No Gina. Brandon's fear returned.

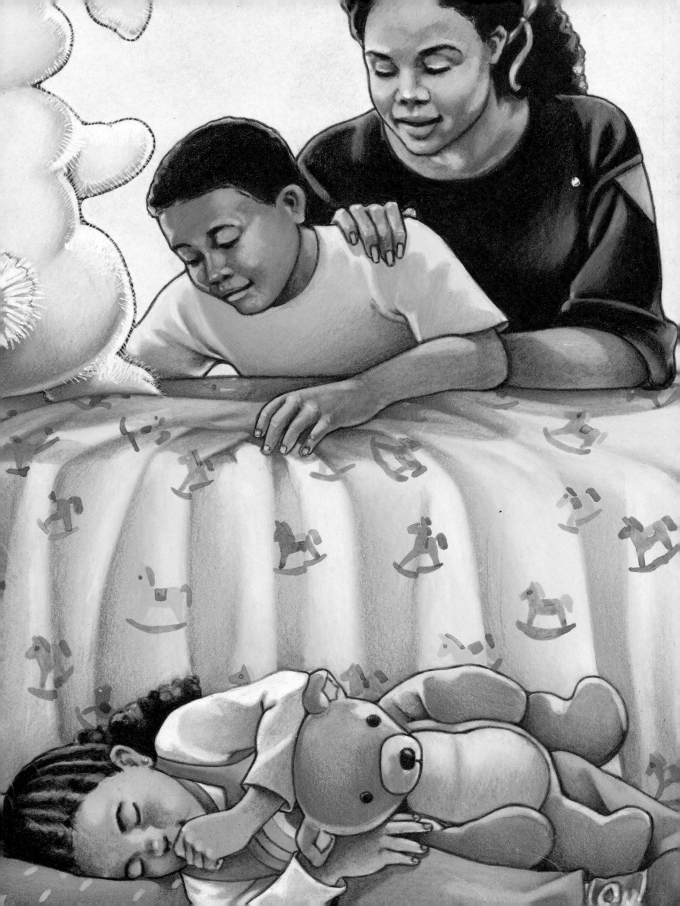

Then he saw something on the floor
between the wall and Gina's bed. His heart
pounded with excitement. He looked more
closely. It was Gina on the floor fast asleep.

"Look at this, Mama," Brandon said. "Here
she is." He was so relieved he wanted to pick
her up and hold her close.

He helped Mama tuck Gina into her bed. When they had quietly closed the door, Brandon said, "Whew! You'll have a lot to swap tonight. She's only two, but she is too much."